Dandelions

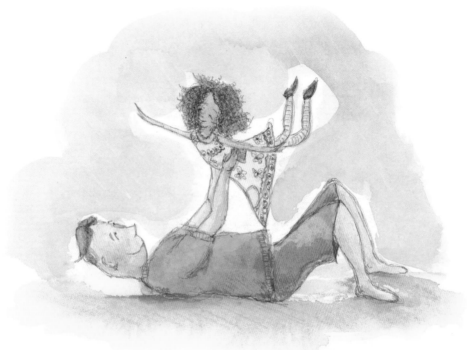

Katrina McKelvey

and

Kirrili Lonergan

'STOP!' I yell, running outside. I'm too late.

'What's wrong?' Dad asks.

'I was waiting for those dandelion flowers to turn into puff balls so I could blow them away.'

'They're just weeds,' Dad replies.

'Not to me!' I cry.

'I love dandelions! The
fuzziness of their petals.
How they're yellow like
the sun. They're magical!'

Dad sits down beside me. 'You look like you're waiting for something,' he says.

'I am. Even though you mowed my favourite flowers, they'll come back. I just have to wait now!'

Dad sighs. 'I'm sorry I cut your flowers, sweetheart …'

'But follow me. I know something that will cheer you up.'

'You're lucky I didn't pull
them out earlier,' says Dad.

'Thanks, Dad. They're beautiful.'

We take a big, deep breath
and blow as hard as we can.
We send every tiny parachute
spinning up, up, up ...

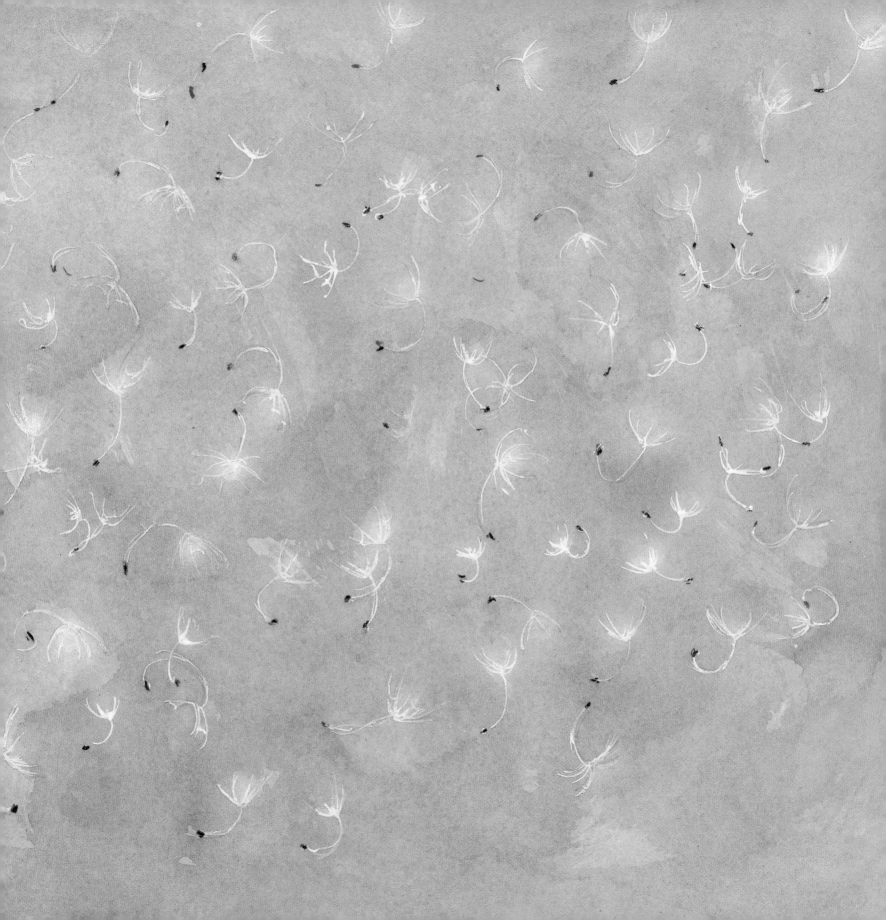

We chase them, running
and panting, until they're
too high to reach.

Exhausted, we flop down on the grass.

As we watch the little parachutes,
we wonder where they go.

Together we imagine them

swirling in the wind

as they pass the roses in our front yard ...

...spinning in the wind

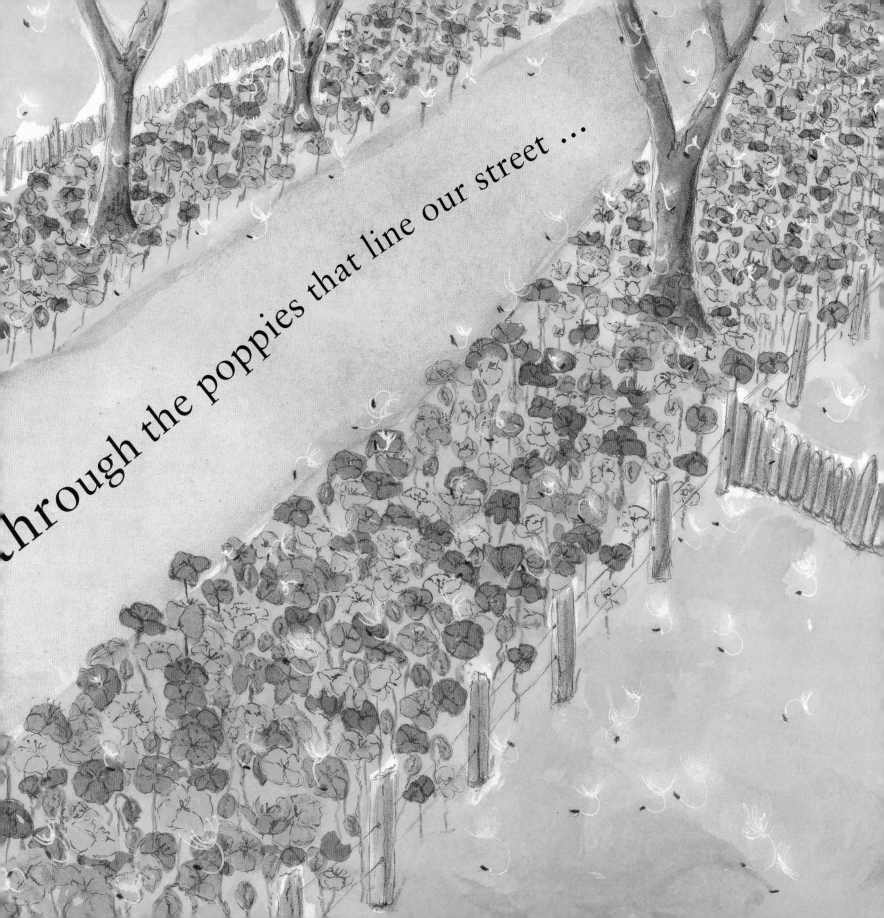

... through the poppies that line our street ...

...twisting in the wind

over the sunflowers in the park ...

... whirling in the win

...ound the weeping willows near the river ...

... turning in the wind under the oak

ree canopies

just out of town . . .

...twirling in the wind between hot ai

alloons bobbing above the countryside and ...

... floating up so high that they're collected by the sun.
Maybe that's why dandelion flowers are yellow.

'Where do they really go, Dad?' I ask.

'After the wind has finished playing with them, they're sprinkled all over the place. Soon new leaves appear, new flowers bloom, and new puff balls grow. Look around!'

'Oh Dad! Now that *is* magic!'

To Alan, Aidan and Lara — what a journey
we are having in this life. Love you! — KM

To my husband and dad — the two best
fathers I know! — KL

First published 2015

EK Books
an imprint of Exisle Publishing Pty Ltd
'Moonrising', Narone Creek Road, Wollombi, NSW 2325, Australia
P.O. Box 60–490, Titirangi, Auckland 0642, New Zealand
www.ekbooks.com.au

A CiP record for this book is available from the National Library of Australia.

ISBN 978-1-921966-82-8

Designed by Big Cat Design
Typeset in Sabon Roman 20/26pt
Printed in China

This book uses paper sourced under ISO 14001 guidelines from well-managed
forests and other controlled sources.

10 9 8 7 6 5 4 3 2 1